The Legend of Sleepy Hollow

WASHINGTON IRVING
illustrated by GRIS GRIMLY

Atheneum Books for Young Readers

NEW YORK † LONDON † TORONTO † SYDNEY

To George Herriman, Winsor McCay,
Lyonel Feininger, Sydney Smith, and
the masters of the early newspaper comics
—G. G.

Atheneum Books for Young Readers
An imprint of Simon & Schuster Children's Publishing Division
1230 Avenue of the Americas
New York, New York 10020
Illustrations copyright © 2007 by Gris Grimly
All rights reserved, including the right of reproduction in whole or in part in any form.
Book design by Ann Bobco
The text for this book is set in Cochin.
The illustrations for this book are rendered in pen, ink, and watercolor.
Manufactured in China
First Edition   OCT 1 7 2007
10 9 8 7 6 5 4 3 2 1
Library of Congress Cataloging-in-Publication Data
Irving, Washington, 1783–1859.
The legend of Sleepy Hollow / Washington Irving ; illustrated by Gris Grimly.
p.   cm.
Summary: A superstitious schoolmaster, in love with a wealthy farmer's daughter, has
a terrifying encounter with a headless horseman.
ISBN-13: 978-1-4169-0625-4
ISBN-10: 1-4169-0625-8
[1. Ghosts—Fiction. 2. New York (State)—Fiction.] I. Grimly, Gris, ill. II. Title.
PZ7.I68Le 2007
[Fic]—dc22   2005027502

Found among the papers of
the Late Diedrich Knickerbocker.

In the bosom of one of those spacious coves which indent the eastern shore of the Hudson lies a small market town, or rural port, which is known by the name of Tarry Town.

Not far from this village, perhaps about two miles, there is a little valley, or rather, a lap of land, among high hills, which is one of the quietest places in the whole world.

From the listless repose of the place and the peculiar character of its inhabitants, who are descendants from the original Dutch settlers, this sequestered glen has long been known by the name of . . .

A drowsy, dreamy influence seems to hang over the land and to pervade the very atmosphere.

Some say that the place was bewitched by a German doctor during the early days of the settlement;

others, that an old Indian chief, the prophet or wizard of his tribe, held his pow-wows there before the country was discovered by Master Hendrick Hudson.

Certain it is, the place still continues under the sway of some witching power that holds a spell over the minds of the good people, causing them to walk in a continual reverie.

They are given to all kinds of marvelous beliefs; are subject to trances and visions, and frequently see strange sights and hear music and voices in the air. The whole neighborhood abounds with local tales, haunted spots, and twilight superstitions.

The dominant spirit, however, that haunts this enchanted region is the apparition of a figure on horseback without a head.

It is said by some to be the ghost of a Hessian trooper

whose head had been carried away by a cannonball in some nameless battle during the Revolutionary War;

and who is ever and anon seen by the country folk, hurrying along in the gloom of night as if on the wings of the wind. His haunts are not confined to the valley,

but extend at times to the adjacent roads and especially to the vicinity of a church. The most authentic historians of those parts allege that the body of the trooper is buried in the churchyard; the ghost rides forth to the scene of battle in nightly quest of his head; and that the rushing speed with which

he sometimes passes along the Hollow, like a midnight blast, is owing to his being belated, and in a hurry to get back to the churchyard before daybreak. The spectre is known, at all the country firesides, by the name of the Headless Horseman of Sleepy Hollow.

The visionary propensity I have mentioned is not confined to the native inhabitants of the valley, but is unconsciously imbibed by everyone who resides there for a time.

However wide awake they may have been before they entered that sleepy region, they are sure to inhale the witching influence of the air, and begin to grow imaginative—to dream dreams and see apparitions. In this by-place of nature, there abode a worthy wight of the name of

ICHABOD CRANE...

who sojourned, or, as he expressed it, "tarried," in Sleepy Hollow for the purpose of instructing the children of the vicinity. He was tall but exceedingly lank, with narrow shoulders, long arms and legs, hands that dangled a mile out of his sleeves, feet that might have served for shovels, and his whole frame most loosely hung together.

His head was small and flat at top, with huge ears; large, green, glassy eyes; and a long snipe nose.

To see him striding along the profile of a hill on a windy day with his clothes bagging and fluttering about him, one might have mistaken him for the genius of famine descending upon the earth, or some scarecrow eloped from a cornfield.

His schoolhouse was a low building of one large room, rudely constructed of logs; the windows partly glazed and partly patched with leaves of old copy-books.

The schoolhouse stood in a rather lonely but pleasant situation, just at the foot of a woody hill with a brook running close by and a formidable birch tree growing at one end of it.

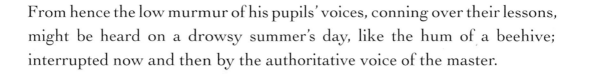

From hence the low murmur of his pupils' voices, conning over their lessons, might be heard on a drowsy summer's day, like the hum of a beehive; interrupted now and then by the authoritative voice of the master.

When school hours were over, he was the companion and playmate of the larger boys, and on holiday afternoons would convoy some of the smaller ones home, who happened to have pretty sisters, or good housewives for mothers, noted for the comfort of their cupboards. Indeed it behooved him to keep on good terms with his pupils.

The revenue arising from his school was small and would have been scarcely sufficient to furnish him with daily bread, for he was a huge feeder, and though lank, had the dilating powers of an anaconda.

But to help out his maintenance, he was, according to county custom in those parts, boarded and lodged at the houses of the farmers whose children he instructed.

With these he lived successively a week at a time, thus going the rounds of the neighborhood with all his worldly effects tied up in a cotton handkerchief.

In addition, he was the singing master and picked up many bright shillings by instructing the young folks in psalmody. Thus, in that ingenious way commonly denominated "by hook and by crook," the worthy pedagogue got on tolerably enough and was thought, by all who understood nothing of the labor of headwork, to have a wonderfully easy life of it.

The schoolmaster is a man of some importance in the female circle of a rural neighborhood, considered a kind of idle gentleman-like personage of vastly superior taste to the rough country swains, and, indeed, inferior in learning only to the parson. His appearance is apt to occasion some little stir at the tea table of a farmhouse, and the addition of a dish of cakes or the parade of a silver teapot. Our man of letters was peculiarly happy in the smiles of all the country damsels. How he would figure among them in the churchyard between services on Sundays, gathering grapes for them from the wild vines that overrun the surrounding trees, reciting for their amusement all the epitaphs on the tombstones; or sauntering with a bevy of them along the banks of the mill pond while the more bashful country bumpkins hung sheepishly back, envying his superior elegance and address.

His appetite for the marvelous, and his powers of digesting it, were equally extraordinary. Both had been increased by his residence in this spellbound region. No tale was too gross or monstrous for his capacious swallow.

A source of fearful pleasure was to pass long winter evenings with the old Dutch wives, as they sat spinning by the fire, and listen to their tales of ghosts and goblins and haunted bridges and particularly of the headless horseman, or Galloping Hessian of the Hollow. He would frighten them woefully with speculations upon comets and shooting stars.

But if there was a pleasure in all this, while snugly cuddling in the chimney corner of a chamber where, of course, no spectre dared to show his face, it was dearly purchased by the terrors of his subsequent walk homeward.

What fearful shapes and shadows beset his path amid the dim and ghastly glare of a snowy night! How often was he appalled by some shrub covered with snow, which, like a sheeted spectre, beset his very path! And how often was he thrown into complete dismay by some rushing blast, howling among the trees, in the idea that it was the galloping Hessian on one of his nightly scourings!

All these, however, were mere terrors of the night, phantoms of the mind that walk in darkness; daylight put an end to all these evils, and he would have passed a pleasant life of it in despite of the devil and all his works if his path had not been crossed by a being that causes more perplexity to mortal man than ghosts, goblins, and the whole race of witches put together, and that was—a woman.

Katrina Van Tassel

Among the musical disciples who assembled one evening in each week to recite his instruction in psalmody, was Katrina Van Tassel, the daughter and only child of a substantial Dutch farmer. She was universally famed, not merely for her beauty, but her vast expectations.

Ichabod Crane had a soft and foolish heart toward the sex; and it is not to be wondered at that so tempting a morsel soon found favor in his eyes; more especially after he had visited her in her paternal mansion.

Old Baltus Van Tassel was a perfect picture of a thriving, contented, liberal-hearted farmer. He was satisfied with his wealth, but not proud of it, and piqued himself upon the hearty abundance rather than the style in which he lived.

Baltus Van Tassel

As the enraptured Ichabod rolled his great, green eyes over the fat meadowlands, the rich fields of wheat, of rye, of buckwheat, and of Indian corn, and the orchards burthened with ruddy fruit, which surrounded the warm tenement of Van Tassel, his heart yearned after the damsel who was to inherit these domains.

From the moment Ichabod laid his eyes upon these regions of delight, the peace of his mind was at an end; he had to encounter a host of fearful adversaries, the numerous rustic admirers who beset every portal to Katrina's heart, keeping a watchful and angry eye upon one another, but ready to fly out in the common cause against any new competitor.

Brom Van Brunt

Among these the most formidable was a burly, roaring, roystering blade of the name Brom Van Brunt, the hero of the country round, which rang with his feats of strength and hardihood. He was broad-shouldered and double-jointed, with short curly hair and a bluff, but not unpleasant, countenance, having a mingled air of fun and arrogance. From his Herculean frame and great powers of limb, he had received the nickname "Brom Bones."

He was famed for great knowledge and skill in horsemanship. He was always ready for either a fight or a frolic, but had more mischief than ill will in his composition; and, with all his overbearing roughness, there was a strong dash of waggish good humor at bottom.

This rantipole hero had for some time singled out Katrina for the object of his uncouth gallantries, and it was whispered that she did not altogether discourage his hopes. Certain it is, his advances were signals for rival candidates to retire.

Such was the formidable rival with whom Ichabod Crane had to contend.

To have taken the field openly against his rival would have been madness. Ichabod, therefore, made his advances in a quiet and gently insinuating manner. Under cover of his character of singing master, he made frequent visits to the farmhouse.

Ichabod would carry on his suit with the daughter under the great elm, or sauntering along in the twilight, that hour so favorable to the lover's eloquence.

Brom, who had a degree of rough chivalry in his nature, would have settled their pretensions to the lady—by single combat. But Ichabod was too conscious of the superior might of his adversary to enter the lists against him. He had overheard a boast

of Bones, that he would "double the schoolmaster up, and lay him on a shelf of his own schoolhouse," and he was too wary to give him an opportunity. Ichabod became the object of whimsical persecution by Bones and his gang of rough riders. They smoked out his singing school by stopping up the chimney; broke into the schoolhouse at night, and turned everything topsy-turvy, so that the poor schoolmaster began to think all the witches in the country held their meetings there. Still more annoying, Brom had a scoundrel dog whom he taught to whine in the most ludicrous manner, and introduced as a rival of Ichabod's to instruct her in psalmody.

In this way matters went on for some time. On a fine autumnal afternoon, Ichabod, in pensive mood, sat enthroned on the lofty stool whence he usually watched all the concerns of his little literary realm.

He was suddenly interrupted by the appearance of a man with an invitation to Ichabod to attend a merrymaking, or "quilting frolic," to be held that evening at Mynheer Van Tassel's. The gallant Ichabod now spent at least an extra half hour at his toilet.

So that he might make his appearance before his mistress in the true style of a cavalier, he borrowed a horse from the farmer with whom he was domiciliated, and, thus gallantly mounted, issued forth, like a knight-errant in quest of adventures. I should, in the true spirit of romantic story, give some account of the looks and equipments of my hero and his steed.

GUNPOWDER

The animal he bestrode was a broken-down plough-horse that had outlived almost everything but his viciousness. Still he must have had fire and mettle in his day, if we may judge from the name he bore of Gunpowder. Ichabod was a suitable figure for such a steed.

He rode with short stirrups, which brought his knees nearly up to the pommel of the saddle; his sharp elbows stuck out like a grasshoppers'; and, as his horse jogged on, the motion of his arms was not unlike the flapping of a pair of wings. A small wool hat rested on the top of his nose, for so his scanty strip of forehead might be called; and the skirts of his coat fluttered out almost to the horse's tail. Such was the appearance of Ichabod and his steed.

As Ichabod jogged slowly on his way, he journeyed along a range of hills that looked out upon some of the goodliest scenes of the mighty Hudson.

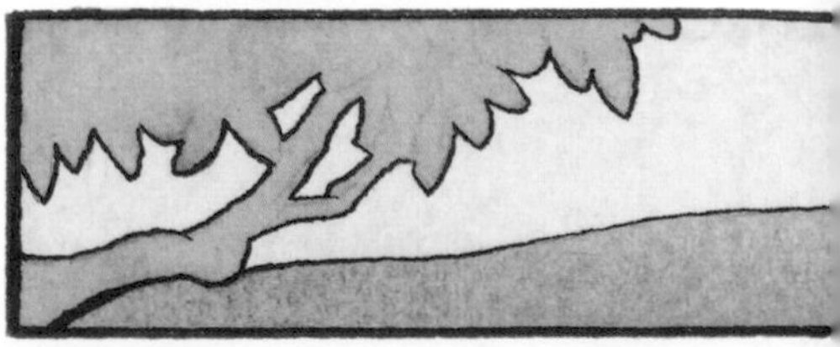

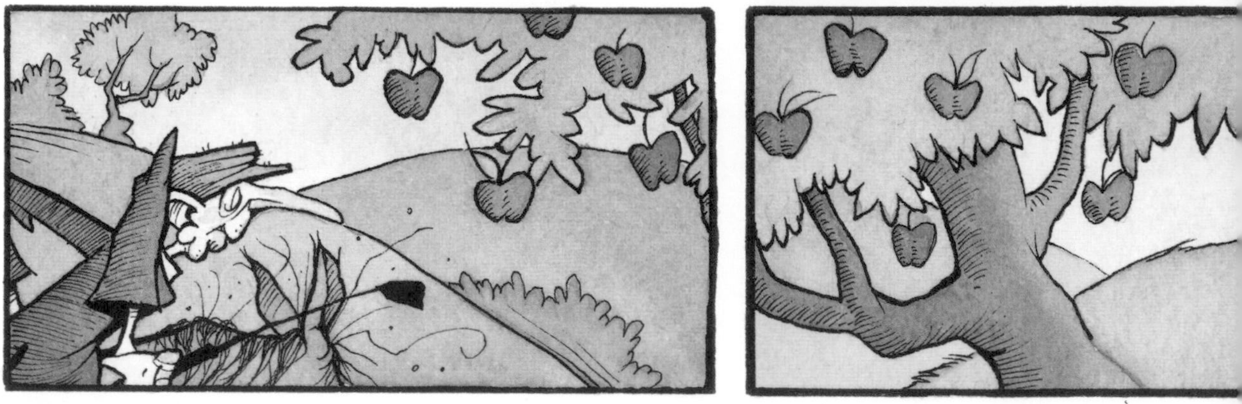

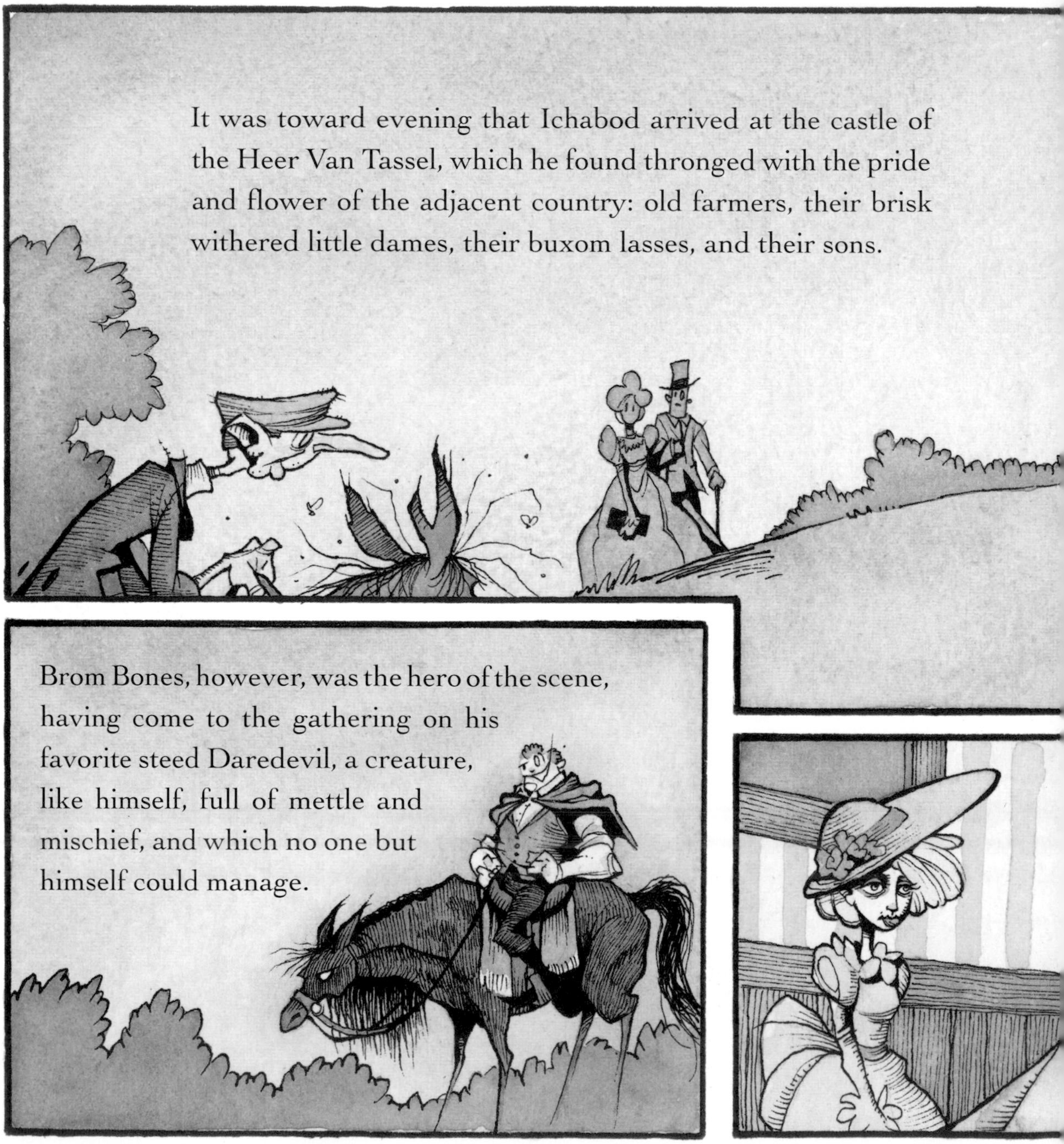
It was toward evening that Ichabod arrived at the castle of the Heer Van Tassel, which he found thronged with the pride and flower of the adjacent country: old farmers, their brisk withered little dames, their buxom lasses, and their sons.
Brom Bones, however, was the hero of the scene, having come to the gathering on his favorite steed Daredevil, a creature, like himself, full of mettle and mischief, and which no one but himself could manage.

And now the sound of the music from the common room, or hall, summoned them both to the dance.

Ichabod prided himself upon his dancing as much as upon his vocal powers. Not a limb, not a fiber about him was idle; and to have seen his loosely hung frame in full motion, and clattering about the room, you would have thought Saint Vitus himself, that blessed patron of dance, was figuring before you in person. The lady of his heart was his partner in the dance, and smiling graciously in reply to all his amorous oglings;

while Brom Bones, sorely smitten with love and jealousy, sat brooding by himself in one corner.

When the dance was at an end, Ichabod was attracted to a knot of the sager folks, who, with old Van Tassel, sat gossiping over local tales and superstitions.

Several of the Sleepy Hollow people were present at Van Tassel's, and, as usual, were doling out their wild and wonderful legends. The chief part of the stories, however, turned upon the favorite spectre of Sleepy Hollow, the headless horseman, who had been heard several times of late, patrolling the country; and, it was said, tethered his horse nightly among the graves in the churchyard.

The sequestered situation of this church seems always to have made it a favorite haunt of troubled spirits. Over a deep black part of the stream, not far from the church, was formerly thrown a wooden bridge; the road that led to it, and the bridge itself, were thickly shaded by overhanging trees, which cast a gloom about it, even in the daytime; but occasioned a fearful darkness at night. This was one of the favorite haunts of the headless horseman; and the place where he was most frequently encountered.

The tale was told of old Brouwer, a most heretical disbeliever in ghosts; how he met the horseman returning from his foray into Sleepy Hollow, and was obliged to get up behind him; how they galloped over bush and brake, over hill and swamp, until they reached the bridge;

when the horseman suddenly turned into a skeleton, threw old Brouwer into the brook, and sprang away over the treetops with a clap of thunder.

This story was immediately matched by a thrice marvelous adventure of Brom Bones, who made light of the galloping Hessian as an arrant jockey.

He affirmed that, on returning one night from the neighboring village of Sing Sing, he had been overtaken by this midnight trooper; that he had offered to race with him for a bowl of punch, and should have won it, too, for Daredevil beat the goblin horse all hollow, but, just as they came to the church bridge, the Hessian bolted and vanished in a flash of fire.

 All these tales, told in that drowsy undertone with which men talk in the dark, sank deep in the mind of Ichabod.

The revel now gradually broke up. Ichabod lingered behind to have a tête-à-tête with the heiress, fully convinced that he was now on the high road to success. Something, however, I fear me, must have gone wrong, for he sallied forth, after no very great interval, with an air quite desolate and chopfallen.

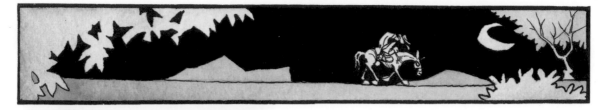

It was the very witching time of night that Ichabod, heavyhearted and crestfallen, pursued his travel homeward. The hour was as dismal as himself. In the dead hush of midnight he could even hear the barking of the watchdog, but it was so vague and faint as only to give an idea of his distance from this faithful companion of man. No signs of life occurred near him.

All the stories of ghosts and goblins that he had heard in the afternoon, now came crowding upon his recollection. The night grew darker and darker. He had never felt so lonely and dismal. He was, moreover, approaching the very place where many of the scenes of the ghost stories had been laid. In the center of the road stood an enormous tulip tree, which towered like a giant above all the other trees of the neighborhood and formed a kind of landmark. Its limbs were gnarled and fantastic, large enough to form trunks for ordinary trees, twisting down almost to the earth and rising again into the air.

As Ichabod approached this fearful tree, he began to whistle; he thought his whistle was answered. It was but a blast sweeping sharply through the dry branches.

As he approached a little nearer, he thought he saw something white, hanging in the midst of the tree. He ceased whistling, but on looking more narrowly, perceived that it was a place where the tree had been scathed by lightning, and the white wood laid bare. Suddenly he heard a groan; and his knees smote against the saddle. It was but the rubbing of one huge bough upon another as they were swayed about by the breeze. He passed the tree in safety, but new perils lay before him.

About two hundred yards from the tree, a small brook crossed the road and ran into a marshy and thickly wooded glen. A few rough logs, laid side by side, served for a bridge over this stream. To pass this bridge was the severest trial. This has ever since been considered a haunted stream, and fearful are the feelings of the schoolboy who has to pass it alone after dark.

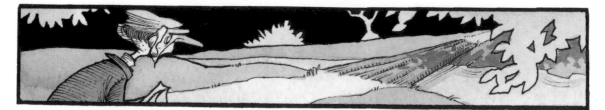

As he approached the stream, his heart began to thump; he gave his horse half
a score of kicks in the ribs, and attempted to dash briskly across the bridge;
bestowed both whip and heel upon the starveling ribs of old Gunpowder, who
dashed forward, snuffling and snorting, but came to a stand just by the bridge,
with a suddenness that had nearly sent his rider sprawling over his head.

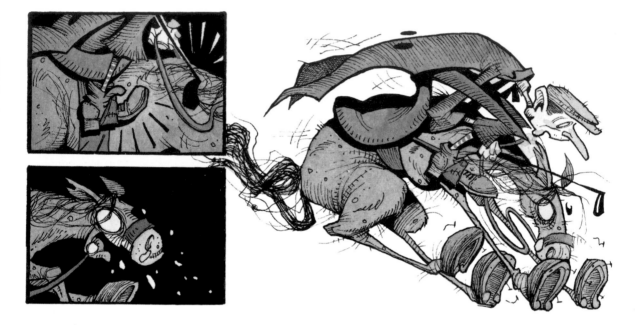

Just at this moment a plashy tramp by the side of the bridge
caught the sensitive ear of Ichabod.

In the dark shadow of the grove, on the margin of the brook, he beheld something
huge, misshapen, black, and towering. It stirred not, but seemed gathered up in
the gloom, like some gigantic monster ready to spring upon the traveler.

The hair of the affrighted pedagogue rose upon his head with terror. What was to be done? To turn and fly was now too late; and besides, what chance was there of escaping ghost or goblin, if such it was, which could ride upon the wings of the wind?

Summoning up, therefore, a show of courage, he demanded in stammering accents — "Who are you?"

He received no reply. He repeated his demand in a still more agitated voice. Still there was no answer.

Just then the shadowy object of alarm put itself in motion, and, with a scramble and a bound, stood at once in the middle of the road. He appeared to be a horseman of large dimensions, and mounted on a black horse of powerful frame. He kept aloof on one side of the road, jogging along on the blind side of old Gunpowder, who had now got over his fright and waywardness.

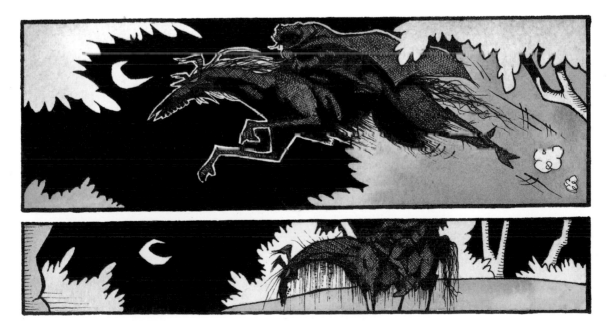

Ichabod, who had no relish for this strange midnight companion and bethought himself of the adventure of Brom Bones with the Galloping Hessian, now quickened his steed. The stranger, however, quickened his horse to an equal pace.

Ichabod pulled up, and fell into a walk, thinking to lag behind, the other did the same. His heart began to sink within him. There was something in the moody and dogged silence of this pertinacious companion that was mysterious and appalling. It was soon fearfully accounted for.

On mounting a rising ground, which brought the figure of his fellow traveler in relief against the sky—gigantic in height and muffled in a cloak—Ichabod was horror-struck on perceiving that he was . . .

headless!

But his horror was still more increased on observing that the head, which should have rested on his shoulders, was carried before him on the pommel of the saddle.

His terror rose to desperation; he rained a shower of kicks and blows upon Gunpowder, hoping, by the sudden movement, to give his companion the slip—but the spectre started full jump with him. Away then they dashed, through thick and thin; stones flying and sparks flashing at every bound. Ichabod's flimsy garments fluttered in the air as he stretched his long lank body away over his horse's head, in the eagerness of his flight.

They had now reached the road that turns off to Sleepy Hollow; but Gunpowder, who seemed possessed with a demon, made an opposite turn, and plunged headlong downhill to the left.

This road leads through a sandy hollow, shaded by trees for about a quarter of a mile, where it crosses the bridge famous in goblin story, and just beyond, swells the green knoll on which stands the whitewashed church.

As yet the panic of the steed had given his unskillful rider an apparent advantage in the chase; but just as he had got halfway through the hollow,

the girths of the saddle gave way, and he felt it slipping from under him

and had just time to save himself by clasping old Gunpowder around the neck when the saddle fell to the earth, and he heard it trampled under foot by his pursuer.

An opening in the trees now cheered him with the hopes that the church bridge was at hand.

The wavering reflection of a silver star in the brook told him that he was not mistaken. He saw the walls of the church under the trees beyond. He recollected the place where Brom Bones's ghostly competitor had disappeared. *If I can but reach that bridge,* thought Ichabod, *I am safe.*

Just then he heard the black steed panting and blowing close behind him; Ichabod even fancied that he felt his hot breath.

The horseman gained the opposite side; and now Ichabod cast a look behind to see if his pursuer should vanish, according to rule, in a flash of fire and brimstone.

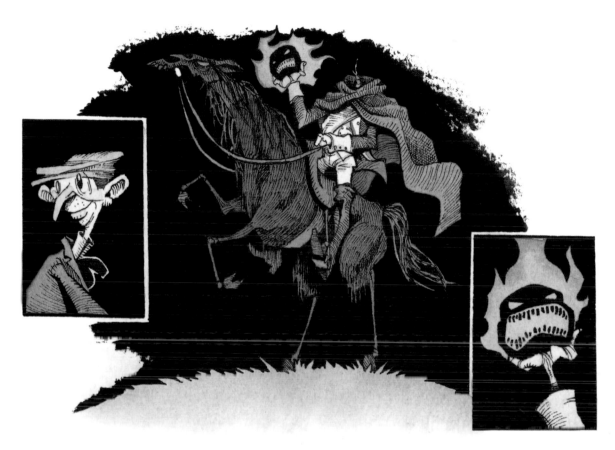

Just then he saw the goblin rising in his stirrups and in the very act of hurling his head at him.

Ichabod endeavored to dodge the horrible missile, but too late. It encountered his cranium with a tremendous crash. He was tumbled headlong into the dust, and Gunpowder, the black steed, and the goblin rider, passed by like a whirlwind.

The next morning the old horse was found without his saddle and with the bridle under his feet, soberly cropping the grass at his master's gate. Ichabod did not make his appearance at breakfast. Dinner hour came, but no Ichabod.

The boys assembled at the schoolhouse and strolled idly about the banks of the brook, but no schoolmaster. An inquiry was set on foot, and after diligent investigation they came upon his traces. In one part of the road leading to the church was found the saddle trampled in the dirt; the tracks of horses' hoofs deeply dented in the road, and evidently at furious speed, were traced to the bridge, beyond which, on the bank of a broad part of the brook, where the water ran deep and black, was found the hat of the unfortunate Ichabod, and close beside it a shattered pumpkin.

The mysterious event caused much speculation at the church on the following Sunday. The stories of Brouwer, of Bones, and a whole budget of others were called to mind. And when they had diligently considered them all and compared them with the symptoms of the present case, they shook their heads and came to the conclusion that Ichabod had been carried off by the galloping Hessian.

It is true that an old farmer, who had been down to New York on a visit several years after, and from whom this account of the ghostly adventure was received, brought home the intelligence that Ichabod Crane was still alive; that he had left the neighborhood, partly through fear of the goblin and partly in mortification at having been suddenly dismissed by the heiress.

Brom Bones, too, who shortly after his rival's disappearance conducted the blooming Katrina in triumph to the altar, was observed to look exceedingly knowing whenever the story of Ichabod was related, and always burst into a hearty laugh at the mention of the pumpkin, which led some to suspect that he knew more about the matter than he chose to tell.

The old country wives, however, who are the best judges of these matters, maintain to this day that Ichabod was spirited away by supernatural means; and it is a favorite story often told about the neighborhood around the winter evening fire of Sleepy Hollow.

The schoolhouse, being deserted, soon fell to decay,

and was reported to be haunted by the ghost of the unfortunate pedagogue,

his voice at a distance, chanting a melancholy psalm tune among the tranquil solitudes of Sleepy Hollow.